MW00809680

Aida

Aida

Airy Ferreras Molina

Columbus, Ohio

This book is a work of fiction. The names, characters and events in this book are the products of the author's imagination or are used fictitiously. Any similarity to real persons living or dead is coincidental and not intended by the author.

The views and opinions expressed in this book are solely those of the author and do not reflect the views or opinions of Gatekeeper Press. Gatekeeper Press is not to be held responsible for and expressly disclaims responsibility of the content herein.

Aida

Published by Gatekeeper Press
2167 Stringtown Rd, Suite 109
Columbus, OH 43123-2989
www.GatekeeperPress.com

Copyright © 2021 by Airy Ferreras Molina
All rights reserved. Neither this book, nor any parts within it may be sold or reproduced in any form or by any electronic or mechanical means, including information storage and retrieval systems, without permission in writing from the author. The only exception is by a reviewer, who may quote short excerpts in a review.

Copyright for the illustration: iStockphoto.com/ Bwiselizzy (Tree of life)
The cover design, interior formatting, typesetting, and editorial work for this book are entirely the product of the author. Gatekeeper Press did not participate in and is not responsible for any aspect of these elements.

Library of Congress Control Number: 2021933600

ISBN (hardcover): 9781662911224
ISBN (paperback): 9781662911231
eISBN: 9781662911248

Contents

Introduction

In memory of the one who pushed me to finish this project!

The day you left us, a part of me died with you, but a new window opened. Life has changed for the better. Now, I appreciate the smallest things in life, enjoy the sun and the rain more than ever, because every part of earth brings me closer to you.

Thank you mi Vieja!

Grandma 2020

How can I . . . how can I forget you? When everything and anything I do, all I can see is you.

How can I forget you, when everything you did was to dedicate your life to your loved ones?

Grandma, it is impossible to let you go when I didn't even have the chance to say goodbye.

I cannot admit you are no longer here. The pain I feel is so heavy, it feels like I can't breathe. I try to fight these smothering emotions, but I can't seem to control them; they are slowly killing me on the inside. I know I won't see you again. If I close my eyes, I hear your voice so clearly, it relieves the pain from my chest. I hear you telling me it is selfish to not say goodbye, it is selfish to not to let you leave and rest in peace. The last thing you would want for me is to harm myself. I have decided to wake up and fight every day. I will continue to spread the love you planted in me. Grandma, even when you are so far away, I can still feel your presence. You give me strength. You give me hope to dream.

Grandma

Your heart was so clear. Your hands were so soft. Your words calmed me down. Now that you are gone, I feel lost. I feel lost, yet I feel you in my heart. I feel your spirit connect with mine. Even when I feel alone, I still feel you close. You are like the wind. Even when I cannot see you, I can still feel you. You are pushing me to do better. Grandma, I will make you proud, and I will take your name to the sky. I will scream your name and your legend will rise, rise so high that heaven will dance. The heavens will dance to the sound of victory over death wrought by love.

The Sky

As I stare at the sky and focus my eyes on the moon, I see so much beyond life. . . . I can picture your face smiling at me. I hear your heart beating so fast. This connection is new to me. I never thought I would feel you with me again, as I hear your voice while my eyes focus on the moon. When I'm walking in the woods, I feel you as the wind dances around my body. I see you in the sky as the birds fly by. Even when it rains, I hear your heartbeat as if you were still with me. Even though this connection is strange and new to me, I am glad to meet you again.

Hi, Grandma

Hi, Grandma. I hope you saw me take another step towards our dream. I just graduated with a bachelor's degree. I hope you are smiling from another life! I wish you were here to hold my hands and to tell me how proud you are of your crazy ñoña. I miss you so much! Besos, from another life.

Grandma's soul has flown to heaven

Life Is Funny

On the road, tripping on rocks. Tripping on love. Losing your thoughts. Fighting for love. Hating your thoughts. Hating the cuts. Hating to trust. What once was love.

Broken

Broken. . . . When your heart beats so quickly that your body freezes. Your mind is gone. You are fighting for air. Tears stain your cheeks. You feel so weak, so weak you can't even breathe, so weak you can't even speak. You are so weak . . . in that moment you can't even think, and simply try to breathe.

January 19

Once you are broken, it's hard to open your heart. It's hard to open the door to somebody else. The pain remains, running through your veins, like a cancer that won't leave your brain. Your pain, your past traumas, lead you to run away from what could be a true love. The idea of love turns to hate. It pushes away your hopes. Once broken, trust and love turn to fear, and close the space in your heart that opened to love. Hate kills the hope of trusting again without the fear of falling into a black hole.

The Evil

You can break from any type of relationship, not just an intimate relationship. Evil tends to take your kindness for weakness. It uses your capability to feel to manipulate your emotions. Your power to forgive is used to make you believe their lies. Your ability to see the good in the evil to make you believe in their sin. False intentions masked by a genuine gesture.

Our Own Weaknesses

We must remember, as humans we all have our own weaknesses and insecurities. What would a table of food look like if every plate were the same? We need to learn to love ourselves and our flaws without comparing them to others. Why care about their opinions of who they think we should be? When you know yourself, no one can tell you who you are, and what needs to be changed in your life.

Remember

I remember the good times where the sun would shine and the birds would sing. I remember the music of the rain; dancing with no pain. I remember running with no shoes; playing with no shame. I remember loving with no pain; caring with no breaks. I remember living with no agony; loving to be brave. That little girl no longer remembers: what once was love, what once was freedom, what once was to live free, with no pain, with no regrets.

Hard to Open Up

It's hard to open your heart when all you have received is pain. When you come across someone who might seem to have the key to your heart, you can't help but run away. Don't feel bad about protecting your hardness, don't feel bad to maintain your doubts towards a new face in your life. Those who love you will prove their worth, their actions will speak louder than their words. To trust your instincts is to know who you are and what you are worth. No one can define you, nor take that right away from you.

Would You

When I hear the word "fighting," I see the evil fighting for my soul. I see the pain provoking my emotions. I see myself battling a broken heart that has suffered multiple stab wounds. It's hard to find my peace of mind. It's hard to feel those butterflies that once shone in my life.

Finding Ourselves

I'm over it. I don't care. It's a new me. These are the lies we tell ourselves when we try to fight what we actually feel. *Are we really over it? Do we really not care? Is it really a new us?* We speak these lies to ourselves as a weak attempt to move on and forget. In fact, this is not us speaking. This is our pain, our regrets, and that girl inside screaming for help. We try to change ourselves to forget the pain, but in the process, we lose ourselves. We forget who we are. We think we are protecting our heart, but in reality, we are hurting ourselves in a way that no one else can see. Little by little, the pain accumulates and turns into anxiety and depression. We turn ourselves into a person that even we don't recognize in the mirror anymore. Long walks on lonely nights provide the only balm for the pain in our heart.

Self-Power

Life teaches you lessons for numerous reasons. Reasons that, in the moment, might not make sense. Life contains more ups and downs than a rollercoaster. Until you learn self-power, find your strength and your values, only then will you understand the deeper meaning of the lessons you've gone through. We have to keep our eyes open. We need to understand the importance of self-respect. If we don't respect and love ourselves before loving anything and anyone else, our hearts will be played with day after day. In life, we must understand that whenever something goes wrong, it's not because we have failed; something better will come. If we don't fail, if we don't make mistakes, we will never find out who we really are. Let the lessons of life guide you, not destroy you.

Ladies

Since when is it okay for a woman to chase a man? Since when did it become okay for a woman to let a man make decisions for her? We need to rise up. We need to stand up. We need to use our power and our knowledge. Let's be independent. Let's be unique. We need to rise up. We must inspire the next generation to be independent and valuable. Don't let a man define you! Don't let a man decide for you! We have power, we are strong, and we are the future.

Selfish

Am I selfish for thinking about myself before thinking about you? Am I selfish for putting my priorities before yours? Am I selfish for putting my mental health before yours? Am I selfish for choosing my family before yours? Am I selfish for working and building my future before yours? If this how you define selfish, I must admit that I am, dear friend.

Kindness

Kindness can cause us to bleed, at the hands of those who never deserved our love. But, dear friend, don't you ever regret being kind. Don't you ever regret extending your hand to a friend. If they fight us with hate, we fight them with love. in the end, kindness always wins. Those who tried to destroy us with evil and hate end up destroying themselves when we hit back with love.

There Is a Limit

There is a limit to being supportive of others. In order for you to help others, you must first take care of yourself. Don't feel guilty for others' problems or their mental health. Don't let others pressure you or make you feel guilty for not yielding every time they scream for your help. You, yourself, and your well-being come first. Afterward, if you can and have the power to help others, then do so. For now, take care of yourself before taking care of someone else. You won't be able to help another individual if you are not at peace with yourself.

I'm Sorry

I'm so sorry that you feel broken. I'm so sorry that you do not love yourself enough to step back and see what others have done for you. I am truly so sorry that you feel empty inside and need to blame others for your pain. I am so sorry that you are broken to the point you believe everyone in life is against you. I am so sorry, but I cannot stand here and let you break me down. I am so sorry that I know who I am and when to move on from what is not right for me. I am so sorry that I won't halt my destiny to make you happy. I am so sorry that I love myself enough to not let you hurt me. I am so sorry that I'm building myself up without letting your words destroy my scale. Yes, I am sorry, but I can't stand here and watch you try to break the both of us.

Sometimes

Sometimes, we can be strangers. We don't recognize the person we see in the mirror. We have lost ourselves. We have let society change us. We are no longer living for us, for our dreams, or for our desires. We live for what the world believes we should be. We shift from dreaming, to pleasing, which leads us to lose track of ourselves. Leading us to bleed . . . bleeding . . . causing us to lose track of the person we once were.

Life as an Elevator

Think of life as an elevator. When we take an elevator, we choose whether we are going up or down. In life, we don't have a choice about taking the elevator, but it is up to us to make the best out our destination. Wherever we go, our destination cannot be changed, but our thoughts and our energy can be shifted. Don't let your downs lower your ups. Make every experience a learning lesson. While on the ride, don't wish or dream that you could change your destination. Let it be a lesson which readies you for the next entrance in life.

The Purpose of Life

What's life without darkness? What would we do if we didn't fight for a better tomorrow?

LIFE. That's life, a climb towards a better future, towards a better you, where you leave behind your name. Everything you do will make a difference. Don't give up when you don't see a change. The world can see your climbs. Your successes will rise. Keep going . . . keep climbing.

Life as It Is

To live, to dream, to hope, the process of wanting to reach the unknown. It's all that makes us HUMAN. Fear is in between us, blocking our view. We fear the unknown, we fear loss, we fear failure. Yet, when we dream, when we believe, when we hope, and when we reach for more, we will create the hunger, the ambition, and the power to run for the unknown. To run for what we are destined to become.

I Try to Play It Safe

I try to play it safe. I try to stay in my lane. There is a burning inside of me begging me to reach the unknown. My body itches as I think of the *what if?* I explore the thoughts of what I know is not the best for me. I have chosen to explore the mystery of the "if." I have decided to reach for what makes me feel the internal burning sensation when the thought passes my mind. I cannot escape the burning inside my body, the itches around my skin, when I think of the places my heart might find.

Airy Ferreras Molina

All I Want

I'm trying to make it out just like you are. All I want is to be free, to fly as fast as I can, with no fear of falling.

2020

Every experience in life is training us to survive. Every situation in life is preparation for the fight to come. Life will throw rocks at us to make us grow and appreciate the beauty of our world. Every broken bone gives us a new perspective of what is to come, it makes us stronger than before. We learn to love, we learn to appreciate the sun, we learn to appreciate every step of towards our destination without regretting every obstacle in our way.

Scared

There is no worse feeling than to feel you won't make it. To be unable to see the light at the end of the tunnel, to walk aimlessly without not knowing your destination. The voice in your head is lying that you won't make it . . . but the power within you pushes, the hunger in your bones makes you wild, and makes you run as fast as you can. Even when you can't see the light, deep down you know the light will be waiting for you at the end of your race. Shine, rise, run . . . for life.

Your Heart

Let your heart feel the pumping blood. Feel the pain tightening in your chest. Feel the pain spreading through your chest. Breathe, just breathe. Turn that pain into your strength. To feel is to obtain the power of self-freedom. Welcome the pain in your life as you fight the burning inside that will eventually make you shine.

DO NOT

We cannot expect anyone else to fight for our dreams. We cannot ignore our desire to live for what we believe. We cannot sleep while the demons defeat our attempt to rise to our feet. We cannot believe it is impossible to dream. When we believe, there is nothing impossible in life. It all seems impossible when we are too afraid to face reality, the reality of true hard work, of showing the part of ourselves we have not revealed to the world.

HANDS

I want to grow. I want to float. I want to reach the top and share my vibe with those who are willing to shine, those who are willing to fly after their life. I am ready to open the door for those who are willing to dance and glow with a purposeful life. Shining, dancing, laughing together as we dance through our life experiencing a unique vibe. Our spirits fly, fly so high, where love beats the odds of the evil eyes around us.

You Want to Do It

Do what you desire. Do what you love. Do what makes you happy. Do not wait for approval: be confident, be your own leader, be your own motivator. Don't let your happiness depend on others. Focus on you. You are responsible for your peace of mind and love. To do what you want is to create your happiness. By creating your happiness, you are creating confidence. By creating confidence, you are creating self-love, and by creating self-love you are choosing to do what you desire to do. Dream what you will without letting any individual voice determine your decisions towards your destination.

Inside of You

There is no worse competition than yourself. That person inside of you telling you, you are not worth it.

YOU

Do you, be you, follow you. You have control of your life. You are the one who knows your way. No one can know you the intimate and authentic way you know yourself.

Feeling

Feeling your emotions is painful. Feeling your emotions can bring you back to a path where you previously shut down. It can open traumas buried underneath mounds of earth. It can open those wounds to bleed again, yet, feeling your emotions can let you clear your heart. It can help you learn how to move on from what once caused you to break, cause you to bleed as if your soul left your body. Feeling your emotions can free you from underneath ground where you buried your pain to avoid causing those wounds to overflow blood.

We Avoid Darkness

We tend to avoid loneliness. We love to love, and to feel loved. We run from darkness and pain. Some of us know how to love, yet in the process of loving we forget to learn to be by ourselves. We forget to learn how to feel pain, how to enjoy the darkness that brings out who we are, and teaches us how to value ourselves and our time. We forget to love who we are. We forget to learn how to walk away from those who push us off of our shelf. We forget to avoid getting hurt, to avoid getting our hope in love destroyed.

It Is Not That We Don't Care

It is not that we don't love or care enough to reach our goals. The real problem is that we tend to get stuck within our emotions. We tend to let our pain stop us from reaching higher. Because we are so afraid to fall, so afraid to get hurt once again, we tend to simply block our way to prevent ourselves from falling. We smile, we love, we care, but we are too afraid to let others love us and care for us. We tend to be as happy and shiny as the sun. We tend to appear as the happiest, yet we are the ones hurting the hardest.

It Is Dangerous to Love

It is dangerous to love someone more than you love yourself. At that point, we tend to love the way we would like to be loved. We forget about our needs, our dreams, our time. We forge their path while ours fades away in front of our eyes. When you love someone, make sure you love yourself enough to step back when your time is required to fulfill your own path!

Stare at the Moon

I stare at the moon and picture myself reaching for more. There is nothing worse than fearing your own dreams. There is nothing worse than thinking those hopes won't carry you past the moon. I see the moon, I see my dreams dancing in the sky waiting for me to fly. I'm ready to fly with the moon guiding my path where I can't yet seem to pass.

Fear

We fear feeling unusual, we fear to fall, we fear to fail. These fears are imposed by those around us. Society has taught us that it is not okay to fall. It teaches us that if we fail, our life will crumble into pieces, BUT the truth is that life would not be life without a fall. Falling, failing, is what helped those on top succeed. Learn from your mistakes. Take the chance to start a new road without letting others decide which side you should drive on.

I Want to Be Able

I want to be able to fly. I want to be able to shine! While walking down the street, I want to smile at the smallest things in life, the smell of flowers, the smell of the rain, the smell of love without the taste of pain.

Reaching

When reaching happiness, we realize the effect energy has on us. We realize the importance of surrounding ourselves with the right people who carry the right energy and and direct pure intention towards us. When healing, the people who carry negative energy will affect our healing process, it will affect the peace we are building towards a happier version of us.

The Law of Attraction

The "Law of Attraction" never lies. It doesn't choose sides. What you put into your head will be the same energy you get in return. Don't focus on the negative. Think positively and create your life in your thoughts the same way you want it to play out.

Yet

—When you find the secret to your happiness, it is hard for others to break that wall. When you find a way of loving yourself, it is hard for others to break your heart. When you learn the truth of love, loyalty, and happiness, it is hard for others to trick you into believing they love you when they don't. Don't be afraid to show your worth, yet do not believe everyone is coming into your life to hurt you. Not everyone is trying to break you down. You will find the balance. You will be able to detect evil from good. Don't settle for less, nor forget about those who have a good heart to lift you higher.

Understanding the Power

Understanding the power necessary to change your life is one of the hardest parts of success. "I believe" is simply not enough. Become your boss, become your motivation, become your competition. Because I can tell you one thing, no one stands between you and your dreams but yourself. Take over your life by learning how to control your thoughts. You can go as far as you want, as long as you are ready for the battle from your own self. It is *you* against *you.*

Hunger

—When you want to succeed, there won't be any other vision but that what you desire. Life gives you options, but you decide the battles you fight. You are driving your bus. You can find your path down the long way as you beat all the odds and doubts you have created, or go the easy way without obtaining what you deserve. Do not settle for less, fight for what you want. Only you have control over what road you decide to take.

Complications

"Life is complicated, it is not perfect. However, it is up to us to learn when we fall." When I asked my father about life, those were his words. He taught me wisdom in my actions and words. Learn how to fall, but most importantly, learn how to walk without looking back at the broken bones from the process of growing into a better person.

It Is Not You

It is okay to be upset. It is okay to show you are hurt. In the process of absorbing the pain, it is important to think of those who hurt you, and the demons they are fighting. Sometimes people react based on their pain or their struggle. IT IS NOT YOU! It is them. It is important to remind ourselves that the actions of others simply reflect their own struggles, their own pain, and the demons inside of them. It is not you, it is THEM.

Just Remember

When the windows are dark and you cannot see the sky, when your life seems on pause as the world spins, when you feel stuck in a deep hole where no one can hear you scream for help, remember this moment will pass. Just remember that it is a moment of doubt. Remember to believe, remember to breathe, and hold on to the hopes deep down your guts. Remember there are those unseen by us yet they can see our pain. They are waiting for us to beat our battle, to walk the path when the clouds clear, allowing us to see our destination at a better time.

It Is Okay to Feel

—It is okay to feel as long as we understand those feelings help us grow into a new person. When we feel, we are becoming unique. Not everyone has the power of taking in their feelings. We appear weak for feeling our emotions, do not let that change you. Your feelings help you escape pain. They help you forgive and love again. They help you understand that it was never you, but the person who hurt you. They did not know who they were, and closed off from their feelings, they hurt you to make you feel "less." Retaliating and making you feel as if your emotions were your weakness. In reality, you are stronger than them, you were not afraid to feel. Don't forget that your feelings will speak to you. They will heal you and lead to you to find your happy place.

Learn

—Learn to not care too much about those who do not treat you with the same caring energy. Sometimes, we get lost in the actions of others when we cannot find an explanation. We need to learn that there is nothing to explain to those who don't care, those who don't see the pain they leave behind. Growing from pain requires us to forget about the actions of others and forgive them without expecting an explanation. They are someone who is lost in their own world.

3:50 a.m.

Just like the mountain, we must be steady and ready for any climb that comes our way without an alarm.

Connecting with the Inner

"Connecting with the inner" is one of the first steps towards setting yourself free. Loving yourself will free you from any depression, or thoughts that guide you to believe you are not enough. Once you learn how to value and love your own self, you free your soul from any negative thoughts.

10/12/2020

Sometimes, we need the rain to appreciate the sun, and just like we need the rain to appreciate the sun, we need the sun to appreciate the rain. Success without pain, freedom without the fight, wouldn't be as sweet, as strong, as beautiful, or as powerful without struggle. We need to sit back and admire our rainy days because those days are what build us, make us humble, and grateful.

You Can Not

You cannot just dream, you must work for the vision. Work like there is no tomorrow! Wake up and chase those dreams without fearing what is yet to come! You are building your own path, you are the one in control. Don't fear the unknown, but don't forget to walk away from the moments that do not fulfill your destiny.

The Sensation of Running

When you have the instinct to run, of chasing for more, don't think twice. Run, run, after that hunger of wanting more. Run as fast as you can until you reach what makes your body itch and won't let you sleep at night. Take the chance, because that dream might not stay awake for too long.

You Know Your Limits

You know your limits. You know your strength. Don't ever let anyone tell you what you can or cannot do. Do what you want, and don't let anyone bring your dreams down or say you cannot reach that high. Remember, the sky is not the limit, the limit is what you set your mind to. Dream, and reach as high as you want. There is a world out there waiting for you, go take over.

Settling

There is nothing wrong with settling, but are you happy where you are? Are you okay with your accomplishments? If the answer is "no," this is when settling down has a negative impact on your life. If you are not happy with what you are doing at the moment, do not stop dreaming and chasing the things you want for yourself. You must remember, we were born on our own and we will die on our own. Live your life as if today was your last day on earth. Chase every opportunity and door that opens up for you. Do what makes you happy, not what makes those around you happy.

On Your Own

Work on you own, put in the work required to get where you want to be. No one else will put in the work to help you reach your goals. Forget about what the world wants and focus on what you need to become a better version of you. Focus on yourself. Don't be afraid to do it on your own.

On the Road

—While on the road, no one will hold your hand, no one will pick you up. But I assure you, once you reach the mountaintop, everyone will claim to know you. So don't be afraid of what they say now. In the end, all the negative talk just confirms you are doing something right.

Energy

Key to keeping our energy balanced is to protect that energy. Surrounding ourselves with those who do not carry the same energy as us harms our peace of mind. Surrounding ourselves with those who carry a negative vibe will unbalance our highs. Surrounding ourselves with people who don't wish us well will hurt our soul. When we understand the effect that energy has in our life, our circle will become smaller, and being by ourselves will not be a scary option, but more of a priority. The energy around us can be absorbed without us realizing the negative impact on our soul.

We All

We all have a dream. Some of us ignore our wishes and desires, but that doesn't mean we do not dream. Don't bury those dreams. Let them come out, let them shine. Whatever you wish for, just know it is not wrong to wish to achieve more.

Be Ready

There is always a light at the end of the tunnel. Being brave and walking the journey will light up your way in the darkest tunnel. Even when it feels you are the only one walking the path, just know *we* are watching your back. Even in the darkest moments you are never alone. Sometimes, all it takes is to believe in ourselves and understand *we* always got ourselves.

Adrenaline

The feeling of knowing you will take steps you never thought you would take must be the worst adrenaline you can experience. However, it is also the strongest happiness you cannot explain. Knowing you are going as fast as a roller coaster, knowing your destination is almost here, can cause us to feel the adrenaline coursing through our body. To know the wind blowing in your favor, clearing your view, can trigger anxiety. Knowing we are arriving at a new beginning is a feeling we cannot explain. Knowing you are approaching the mountain summit can be the best, strongest adrenaline our body can feel.

To Be Afraid

To be afraid is part of knowing you are doing what you really want to do. Don't let your thoughts guide you in the wrong direction. If you know you want it, don't be afraid to grab it. It is better to try than be sorry. At the end of every experience, there's a reason behind it. Shoot your shot.

Sometimes

Sometimes, it is your own family who lets you down. It is hard to walk away from the people who saw you grow into the person you are now. But, it is worse to stick around and let those people bring you down by not believing in your power to change your life. If you change the traditions that run in your family, it is scary to think you are the one to break this cycle, isn't it?

It Will Be Hard

I created a path for myself, and it will be hard for others to destroy my vision. Yet there will be those who attempt to break me down without any caution signal. Those are the ones that will build me up and create the stronger person I will be tomorrow.

December 2020

I see so much of you when I look at you. When I stare into your eyes, I can see your pain, and somehow my own pain reflects back on me. I don't know whether I'm feeling love or whether we have found comfort in between us?

Afraid

Maybe I should tell him that I like him, but I'm afraid of what he's thinking in his head. I'm afraid to love again, but mostly I'm afraid to be broken again!

In My Bed

As I sit in my bed, I can't stop thinking of him. I'm not quite sure what is it that attracts me to him. Could it be his eyes? Could it be his smile? Maybe it is the way he touches me when he speaks? I'm not quite sure, but I know I cannot let him in without not knowing where his heart is!

Crumbling

My emotions seem to crumble. They crawl all over my body, leaving me behind with no body. I cannot seem to choose between the sour and the sweet. I keep going back to those old memories where my heart kept bleeding. Now that I'm stuck in that past moment, I can't seem to accept the feeling of my heart beating without any bleeding.

Pain

I'm hurt. I feel my body crumble under my bed covers. I feel the tears coming down my cheeks. I feel the pain traveling through my veins. Yet, somehow, I see your eyes honey-clear. My heart wishes to feel your body touching, rubbing my skin, as I beg for more from your mystery-love.

Stuck In Between

I seem to have it all. I have found the one to give it all. For once, I have found true love, where the roses are red and the rainbow comes out. I finally discover what love can offer. Yet I'm somehow still stuck on your dangerous touches, where the roses are black, and the rain has no stop. Where your love doesn't reach my heart, yet I'm stuck on the *what if he comes around and switches the cards?*

Between Needs and Wants

There is a difference between "needing" and "wanting." Many times, we confuse "wanting" with "needing." Do not confuse the truth with the lies by sugar coating it. It was never what you needed, but what you wanted. You know it was never for you to begin with, it was simply a desire, not a need.

They Might Think

They might think I'm stupid: stupid for feeling, stupid for pursuing my desire to be bigger than what they portray me to be, but I don't want an apology. I want what I deserve: peace, love, and my wealth. There is no need to feel sorry for me: I'll carry my bag of pain, I'll carry my struggle, and all the stabs I received along the way to better myself. I won't look back nor do I need to hear from any broken promises of the past.

A River of Pain

A river of pain flows through my veins, an ocean of pain fogs my eyes, a tree grows inside my heart binding tight these wounds. Yet my smile portrays a beautiful, happy person for everyone to see. No one can reflect the pain that is floating through my brain. The fight my heart goes through daily to make sure I don't fuck up again. Trying not to let my guard down for any other broken promise, for any other disappointment, for any other broken heart. This fight is between me, myself, and I, because there is nobody to help put the pieces of my heart together again.

A Fight Between My Heart and Brain

There is a constant fight between my heart and my brain. My heart wants to feel love again, but I can't afford for someone else to walk out of my life without any explanation. *Would you hold my hand? Would you make me yours? Would you hold it down the way I would for you?* I'm not sure you can carry me the way I have carried myself and that is what holds me back from loving you and letting you love me the way I have learned to love myself.

Prove Me

I work too hard to let someone walk all over my dignity. When you provide me the respect I deserve, I'll try to check you out. Other than that, peace out!

Don't Tell

Don't tell someone you feel them when you cannot even hear them. Don't tell someone you love them when you cannot even understand them. Your energy speaks louder than your words. Not everyone buys people's words of "kindness" to hide what they really feel. Showing your honesty and revealing your true emotions will forever make others grateful for your ability to keep it real.

I Do Not

Your fakeness does not fit in my circle. I do not suffer hypocrisy. Show me you love me, and I will grant you the world and beyond. Truth is the best medicine to get to my heart.

Dad

You have created a human who can love but defend herself when needed. You showed me what love looks like and the respect I deserved. Because of you, there is no man that can walk into my life without providing me with the right love and respect you have created for me.

Do Not Take My Kindness for Weakness

There is no space for hate in my heart. There is no regret for loving as fiercely as I do. There is no losing when giving it all. At the end of the story, the only person loosing is you when misjudging my kindness for weakness. There is no return when you don't portray the same energy back as when we first started our journey. Once you fuck me over, there is no turning back to the old good times.

Sweet

Sweet, light sugar, smooth like honey, yet free like a butterfly, so be gentle when you handle my love. I'm not afraid to fly away when the rainbow comes out.

Star

The stars will always shine, even when we don't see them, they still shine. Don't be discouraged when going through a hard moment. When you learn to find the positive in the negative, you will be able to shine even when the lights are off.

I Want to See You Shine

I am in love with who I am. I want to see you shine the way I shine even when I'm not around to see it. I want you to learn how to love yourself the way I have learned to love myself. Once we both learn self-love, the love we can share with each other will be impossible to replace. I'll keep shining for the both of us, until you find your way to the real you. Fly my love.

Don't Go Back

Don't permit yourself to go back to what you know you don't deserve. It is easy to fool yourself this is the last time. Walking away from what no longer serves you is hard enough. Don't let yourself believe that this time will be different. You know that "one last time" can turn into another try. So, walk away without looking back at what you know has no exit, no remedy, or solution. Save yourself the unnecessary pain.

"Unfuck Yourself"

Have you heard of the phrase "unfuck yourself?" It is as simple as it sounds. Stop looking back at things that did not happen in your favor or what you did not achieve. Fuck all that! Move forward stronger than yesterday and focus on the new version of yourself. Don't complicate life more than it is already. In life, everything is how we decide to see it. Focus on the highest level of acceptance, and you will reach things beyond what you thought you could achieve. Stop fucking yourself over.

Self-Love

Many don't believe in self-love, they don't believe that one can be so deeply in love with themself. But I must confirm to you, there is no better feeling than loving yourself the way you would want to be loved. Not loving yourself is simply a reflection of the fears you hide behind that smile. We must learn to see reality and accept pain the way it is present in our life. Learning to take that pain in will help you grow into the person you never thought you could be.

The Relationship with Yourself

There is a relationship that you must build with yourself before offering anyone a part of you. There are demons we must fight before helping others defeat theirs. There is pain we must learn to bear before offering a shoulder for others to cry on. There is a whole person inside of us that we must meet before introducing ourselves to any other individual.

Insecurities

Insecurities can be dangerous. They can make us hate and they can stop us from reaching for the things we desire. Insecurities are our biggest enemy and that is why we must learn to love each part of ourselves without reflecting on what could have been. We need to learn to love what we already have. Believe me, there are worse things we could be facing.

We Forget

Sometimes, we forget about our dreams to instead give those we love what they are reaching for. We protect the ones we love by giving every part of us to complete their heart. We give them happy moments to delete their pain. We stop them from bleeding without realizing we are breaking our heart in pieces, causing us to start bleeding, breaking, loosing each part that completes our heart.

Society

When we put aside the things we love, the things we dream of, to do what we think is right in the eyes of those who track our steps, we diminish ourselves. The hurtful truth is that we set aside what we want because society told us to do so. Take a step back and picture yourself achieving your dreams. Can you see yourself happier than you are now? Then go with it, do what you dream all alone! It will feel worse that you never tried what makes you happy because others told you it was the wrong thing to do. You know your heart. Please yourself before pleasing others.

Break It

When you want to be great, nothing will come in between your desires. Every obstacle that comes your way, you must break it. It is your duty to remove and break everything that comes in-between you and your dreams to be "more." When something breaks you down, it is your duty to rebuild yourself and start stronger than before.

Airy Ferreras Molina

I Love You

"I love you" are the three words my daughter tells me when she wakes up, when she eats, and as she lies down next to me. "I love you" are the three words she chooses to tell me. I have to give it all, I have to reach my goal. I have to set the ladder for my little star that is growing under my eyes. She loves me without expecting a thing back. It is my duty to give it all for her, it is my duty to set a clear vision in front of her, it is my duty to demonstrate to her what love can be and what it can do when we love as hard as we do.

Don't

Don't let your fear, don't let your weakness, don't let your downs determine how your future plays out. When you come across these negative thoughts and hard moments, reflect, take a step back, and remind yourself of who you are and who you will become. Those moments of pain, struggles, and weakness will be the tools you need to become the future you. Control your mind, don't let your mind control you.

Feel It

If you want to cry, go ahead and cry. You fell down and broke yourself? Feel the pain. You feel alone and that no one is supporting your thoughts? Well, feel that too. But do not stop from walking and reaching for the moment you have been waiting for. Do not let the world or anyone around you determine who you are. Cry if you need to, feel the pain, but get your ass up and do what it takes to build what you started. No one cares about your pain, your fears, or your struggles. The only one that can determine where you will go is you. You want it, go grab it. Do whatever it takes to break all those moments of doubts.

It Is Okay

It is okay to cry. It is okay to feel the pain we encounter. Tears are a form of release for all the pain that builds inside of us. Cry all you need. In the process of releasing the pain, don't forget who you are and where you have to be. In the process of building yourself, moments of pain and fear will come your way. Those moments do not define you or make you weak. Those moments of pain are important, forcing you to rebuild yourself into a bigger, stronger, and sweeter person.

Stay Ready

You have to stay ready for the unexpected, for the hit in life you were not expecting. You have to be ready for the stab you were not anticipating from the pain you did not create. You have to stay ready for any step of the way where life throws a rock at you without a heads up. That is life. You have to fight any battle that comes into your life, that might make you lose control, or lose your mind. You have to be ready for any fights that come your way.

Delicious

Mom, I thank you for loving me. I thank you for showing me that life is more than what we see. I thank you for opening my wings. Even when you showed me you didn't believe in me I could still feel the love of the mother who showed me how to fly, but feared to let me fly past the sky.

Bitter

Bitter is never better than sweet. I'm sorry that you feel that we are on this road in competition. I'm sorry that you can't see I'm here offering a hand your way. I'm sorry, but I have to pass this road because better things are waiting for me on the other side and I cannot get stuck letting you hold us back. I will pray for you and wait for you when you are ready to love, fly, and take a ride in search of a good vibe, where all we can see are the color of the flowers and birds singing for life.

Trust

A little sister becomes part of your life. When you were born, you came into my life as the one I knew I would have to fight, but even still you brought a kind of happiness I never knew. I have to thank God for sending you my way because you have shown me the value of friendship, trust, and most importantly, the value of chasing my life. Thank you, BIBI. I love you.

Being Alive

Being alive is a blessing many take for granted. We all suffer, and we all struggle. Mine are no worse than yours, and yours are no worse than mine. Our struggles are not to be compared to any other person's struggles. We all have one life to live! Excuses are the only things we all have in common. The power and hunger to change is the difference we all bring to the table. Now, how bad do you want it? If you want it more than life, then there won't be any excuse to say you cannot achieve it. Take it while you breathe, because one thing I can guarantee you is that we all stop breathing, and that has no known due date or time. Spend each day as if it were your last day to live.

Handling Life

In the process of dealing with life, I learned two things. To not give a fuck about irrelevant things and to not pay attention to time because it is one of the biggest excuses. We can rationalize in our head how to feel less guilty about our actions and decisions. It is important to learn how to deal with your struggles and your pain. Trust the process. Time is just a machine to make us feel on track, but there is no such thing as timing when it comes to yourself and the process of working on you.

Your Energy

Your energy is what builds you. It transforms you into the person you are. You have to understand that you are not defined by your body and your thoughts. You are living with a power of energy that defines you and assures you of who you are. Do not let negative vibes and fake people draw you towards a false reflection of who you are not. Your worth and your self-value will never be taken away from you. Hold yourself up, hold your spirit, and your energy high enough where no one and nothing can define you or change you.

Our Own Enemy

Don't fall asleep on yourself. There is no worse enemy than our own selves. To understand who we are and to represent our values is a daily challenge in life. Do not be hard on yourself and do not pay attention to what the world wants from you. Stop and ask yourself *what do I want? What does it take for me to grab that?* Answer these questions and chase what you deserve. No one will give it to you, you must earn it, fight for it, and own it.

The Energy Around Us

Are you feeling like you are losing it? Like there is no way out? Look around you and observe what type of energy is making you feel low. Sometimes we forget the power of the energy around us. We have to be awake at all times. We have to watch our back for those who do not want to see us succeed. It is easy to consume negative energy. Don't accept less than what you deserve. It does not take someone to tell you they don't like you to affect your level of peace. The energy they bring around you will be enough to affect your peace of mind and unbalance your spirituality.

Do Not Regret

Do not regret loving. Do not regret doing better for others. When we decide to do good and help others without expecting anything in return, we will obtain more than what we can see from the universe. Remember that those who hurt us and take our love for granted simply do not have self-love or respect for themselves. In the end, we don't lose, we win. We win certainty and peace in our heart to know we did our part. It is on them to figure out what they are missing. We did not lose love, they did. They lost the love and the world we provided to them that will no longer be available for them to obtain.

Don't Love Me

Don't love me for what you see. Don't love me for what you feel. Don't love me for what you believe I deserve. If you decide to love me, I want you to see through me. I want you to see my soul, my spirit, my energy. I want you to relate to what I'm speaking about. I want you to grow with me. I want you to see beyond life and enjoy every part of you without feeling any type of responsibility from me or for me.

Loving

You do not need to feel bad for others nor should you expect others to feel bad for you. When you love someone, feeling bad is not the way to love them. Giving someone a hand when they fall demonstrates our love. Giving others their space to grow and develop into a better person is loving them. Understanding that our happiness does not depend on the one we love is truly loving them. Love does not expect anyone to carry another's pain, but to grow, and guide them when they need a hand without taking any responsibility for their process of healing their pain.

Our Heart

Our hearts tend to stop when things don't seem to be moving, but isn't that the best part of growing? Knowing that we are feeling and growing even when we don't think we are? We tend to feel the pain of developing our path and that provides reassurance that we are growing. Do not be so hard on yourself. Know that things will fall into place when the work is done. Do not rush the process, and instead learn how to enjoy the journey.

Just Do It

Do what you have to do. Move how you want to move. Speak what you feel. At the end of the day, they all think they know what you do, how you move, and how you feel.

It Is Hard to Love

To give love is hard. It is hard to love when others tend to project their pain on you, but do not get stuck on their false projection. Sometimes, we have to remember that when one is upset and angry, they project a part of them when they speak. They hurt others with their words, but all they are really doing is expressing their own pain and insecurities. Do not get caught up in moments of anger. When someone speaks with anger, it is better to ignore their actions till they stop bleeding a little. Fighting with someone who is hurt won't do much but make things worse. Reflect before you speak.

Do Not Follow

It is hard to ignore those who use their words to hurt you, but it is worse to respond to negativity and poison words aimed to hurt. Do not respond to negative energy. Pray for those who are hurting and pray for their healing. Do not level up to their negative energy. Protect your energy by walking away from situations where there is no answer to be given. They don't need an answer from you, but instead need a hand; a hand of help, a hand that shows what it looks like to be kind to oneself. It is not you, it is them. Listen and ignore the negativity by replacing it with positivity to guide them and make them see the truth without a fight involved in the process.

When Hurting

When people hurt others, it is simply a cry for help. They are hurting, they are broken, and at times they feel the world is against them. We can only offer a hand, guide them to open their eyes, and see the positive side of life. Not everything is grey. Showing someone kindness and love can help turn their world around. As long as your peace has not been disturbed, it is okay to give a hand to those who are in need of help.

Notes to the "Old Me" If I Could Give Myself Advice

Those nights of tears, those nights of fighting the demons will be the moments that reveal the bigger picture of today. Do not regret every broken step you take.

Every mistake, every broken heart, every stab in the back, will be needed to build you into the boss person you will be tomorrow. I would take you back and relive those moments if necessary. Without pain and without betrayal, the window of truth and the real world would not be open, and for that, be thankful for every broken moment you endure in life.

The truth is, that even if you warn yourself not to do something you would likely do it again. Therefore, to the "old me," I would tell you "do it" because you are going to do it anyways. We learn from our mistakes and that is something we cannot avoid. Own every mistake and every wrong step of the way.

Looking back at the "old me," I would admonish myself to not fear change. Don't be afraid of tomorrow. Life is too short and being afraid simply blocks the blessings from walking into your life. Don't be afraid of living the way you want to live.

To the "old me," don't be afraid to love. Don't be afraid to help those who did not return the same love and energy. Giving without expecting anything in return is one of the best forms of love you can provide to yourself.

Understand that the pain of others is not your pain. Their trauma is not yours to fix. Their misunderstanding of who you are is not for you to prove wrong. It is a step that will set you free from toxic relationships.

At some point, depression and anxiety will be your enemy. You will feel you are constantly fighting yourself on a daily basis, but you will win that fight and learn how to control your life and emotion. Those fights will help you grow. Do not regret those fights between your depression and anxiety, because they confirm the strong person you will be tomorrow.

CPSIA information can be obtained
at www.ICGtesting.com
Printed in the USA
LVHW011026160322
713596LV00004B/88